# A TIN TRAIN CHRISTMAS

*a holiday short story*

by Melanie Lageschulte

A Tin Train Christmas
© 2017
by Melanie Lageschulte
Fremont Creek Press

978-0-9988638-4-9 (Kindle ebook)
978-0-9988638-5-6 (paperback)
978-1-952066-22-1 (large-print paperback)

This is a work of fiction. Names, characters, businesses, places, events and incidents are either the products of the author's imagination or used in a fictitious manner. Any resemblance to actual persons, living or dead, or actual events is purely coincidental.

Cover photo: TiSanti/iStock.com
Web: fremontcreekpress.com

# WELCOME!

If you've read any of the "Growing Season" novels, my modern-day series about life in and around the fictional small town of Prosper, Iowa, then you've already met Horace Schermann.

The novels focus on Melinda Foster, who grew up in the Prosper area before moving to the Twin Cities for college and a successful career in marketing and public relations. When Melinda loses her job and a family emergency calls her back to Iowa, she rents Horace's farm for the summer while he stays with his brother, Wilbur, who is in a nearby nursing home.

The Horace in the novels is much older than the one we meet in this short story. In "Growing Season," he's nearly ninety, a lifelong bachelor, intelligent but shy, and someone who loves animals ... especially his dog, Hobo. Here, he's a young boy struggling with his lofty expectations for Christmas and the harsh realities of the Great Depression.

The idea for this short story arrived as I drafted a chapter in "The Peaceful Season" where Horace reminisces about Christmases past. The chance to dive into a project of short fiction that would allow Horace to shine, and bring Wilbur and the rest of their immediate family into focus, was something I couldn't pass up. "A Tin Train Christmas" also lets us visit little Prosper in its heyday, when it was a bustling hub for farmers from miles around, and drop in at the hardware store Melinda Foster's family has operated for decades.

The "Growing Season" series has since evolved into ten titles, and wrapped up with the publication of "Firefly Season" in the fall of 2021. The books are available in several formats, including Kindle editions, paperbacks and hardcovers, and even large-print paperbacks.

Horace is in every book, in one way or another, and Wilbur makes appearances from time to time. Many of the themes present in the novels resonate here as well: family, friendship, faith, and community. At the heart of all these works of fiction, long or short, is the Schermann farm, which provides a place of shelter and love for several generations of one Iowa family before it offers Melinda the thing she needs most: a fresh start.

And if all the references to good food make you hungry, don't worry. At the end, you'll find recipes for three dishes mentioned in the story. They have been handed down in my family, and are a special part of our holiday celebrations.

So grab a cup of coffee or tea, and snuggle in. I hope this short story can, in some way, bring warmth and light to your holiday season. Enjoy!

*Melanie*

# ONE

When the icicles began to stretch from the steep eaves of the farmhouse's roof, and Father needed a lantern to complete evening chores, Horace knew Christmas was only a few weeks away.

Horace Schermann was barely six that winter of 1932, and the wooden-handled snow shovel he pushed and lifted, pushed and lifted along the back steps was almost as tall as he was. It was a wonder he could work the shovel at all, as Mother had him bundled in so many layers of flannel, denim and wool that he could barely toddle about.

This annoyed Horace, as it made him feel like a baby and he wanted to be a big man like Father, or at least as strong and worldly as his older brother, Wilbur, who was in the barn that very moment tossing grain and hay to the horses, cows and sheep, right at Father's side.

Horace sighed and pushed his woolen stocking cap up enough to peer out at the gray expanse of the rural Iowa landscape. When the ground was blanketed with snow and the sun didn't shine, it was as if the sky had no end. If it weren't for the deep gray-green of the shingles on the white farmhouse's roof, or the cheerful red paint on the barn and outbuildings, there would be no color left in the world except for the drab brown of the bare-limbed trees that shivered in the wind.

He'd better get these steps clear and move on to the sidewalk, Horace decided, returning to his task. After that, the chickens needed to be fed, breakfast eaten, and he and Wilbur had to set out on their half-mile walk to school.

That thought actually made him smile. He loved school, loved to read, and was first in his class. He could barely wait for next week's Christmas program, as he was the youngest pupil at the Fulton Township No. 5 school to have a speaking part.

So why wasn't he more excited for Christmas? Horace mulled this over as he worked. Like always, Mother asked him to mark off the days on the calendar tacked up by the kitchen stove, and Father reminded them there would be a Christmas tree with candles at church and lots of homemade cookies.

But something was going on behind Mother and Father's smiles, something didn't seem right. He knew there wasn't much money, but hadn't it always been that way? Horace wasn't sure what had gone wrong, or if he was just getting old enough to better sense what was happening around him, but the idea of Christmas felt different this year.

\* \* \*

He hadn't been too concerned until last night, when he and Wilbur were sandwiched between their feather mattress and layers of quilts with only their noses exposed to the icy air in their bedroom, which was tucked up above the kitchen.

Their grandfather had built the house years ago with a chrome-trimmed coal furnace in the cellar and fancy iron grates in all the floors, but the bedrooms' vents hadn't been opened that fall. Wilbur seemed to know why, but Horace had been too afraid to ask.

Wilbur was eight, and he enjoyed taking charge. That included being the one to carry up the boys' heated flatiron from the sitting-room fireplace and wedge it under the quilts so each boy could, at the very least, get one foot as close to it as possible.

Wilbur, with his extra two years of life experience, also relished being the one to decide when it was time to blow out the kerosene lamp on the little table by their iron-frame bed.

"Well, I don't know how to tell you this, Horace," Wilbur had said, his resigned tone a near-perfect replica of the weary voice Father used all-too-often lately. "But I think it's going to be a lean Christmas. I heard Mother and Father talking in the kitchen just now, when I was warming up the flatiron."

"What did they say?" Horace had tried to turn toward his brother, but the thick stack of blankets nearly pinned him to the mattress. On one hand, Wilbur's proclamation made his stomach drop. On the other, getting a glimpse into the mysterious world of grownups was always interesting.

"I heard Mother say the loan is due in January. You know, the one they had to get after the old well pump broke last summer. Something always seems to be breaking down around here." Wilbur sighed and shook his head.

"So then Father said, 'Well, I think we can cover it, but there's no money for anything else. That means Christmas, too.' About that time is when I bumped into the wood box, and they suddenly got quiet."

"Your cover was blown," Horace had whispered urgently. "It was time to make your escape."

Wilbur had just received the latest issue of his boys' detective magazine, and the brothers had been poring over the stories of mayhem and suspense. On their walks to and from school, they checked for mysterious tracks along the creek and imagined bandits hiding out in the woods.

"So, you know what that means." Wilbur sighed. "That train we saw in the catalog? The one we showed to Father? We're not going to get it."

Horace gasped. "But Wilbur, Santa is the one that brings our toys! Father and Mother get us the other stuff, like the candy and mittens."

Wilbur had been silent for a moment. He'd made a shocking discovery last Christmas, one Father and Mother made him promise to keep to himself. Their little sister Lydia was not yet two, so it didn't matter to her, but Horace ... he was so trusting, he looked up to Wilbur.

Wilbur wished he wasn't so sleepy, that he would have framed his words differently. Disappointment was already weighing on his young heart. If he could spare his brother the worst of it, he would.

"Horace, sometimes Santa doesn't have a lot of money to ... well, buy the materials he needs so the elves can make all the toys." Wilbur warmed to his story.

"Yeah, like that train? That tin and stuff gets expensive, there's a shortage this year, I think. Saw it in the newspaper. But there's always lots of wood, there's a massive forest at the North Pole. So ... Santa can still bring us stuff, just maybe some different stuff. You know what I mean?"

"I guess so." Horace furrowed his brow. "Thanks for telling me. Now I won't be disappointed. Good night."

Wilbur rolled over and fell fast asleep, his conscience cleared, but Horace couldn't seem to close his eyes. Would Santa really leave them off his list this year? How could that be? It made him feel sad and sick at the same time. Just as he had the other day, when he went down to the cellar to get an apple and came upon Mother intently studying the supply of coal.

He'd asked her if something was wrong. But Mother had just wiped her eyes with her apron and took him in her arms. She'd said as long as she had her 'three men,' as she called them, and her little girl, she could face whatever came her way.

Much later, while he was tossing corn to the chickens, it crept up in his mind that, for what had to be the first time ever, Mother hadn't assured him everything was going to be all right.

Horace stared at the plaster ceiling above his head, at the spot where a small dark stain told tales of a leak in the roof. The heavy curtains Mother had made from worn-out quilts covered the two windows from view, but he knew Jack Frost was already etching his designs on their glass.

"This amazing train has a gilt-edged engine," he whispered, quoting the advertisement in the catalog. Horace and Wilbur had spent what seemed like hours running their hands over the illustration, all but willing the train to steam to life and leap off the page. Its track fairly sparkled under the electric lights of a lavishly decorated Christmas tree, and there was a boy in fancy knicker pants crouching nearby with a look of awe and pure joy on his face.

"Its speed is lightning fast, and its engine so powerful, that it'll delight any boy who finds it under the tree ..." Horace at last felt his eyelids grow heavy with sleep. He drifted off to the hum of the winter wind rushing around the corners of the house.

# TWO

Anna Schermann had the coffee pot perking on the back of the kitchen range by the time she heard Henry and the boys come in from morning chores.

"It's a blessing that coffee is still cheap," she comforted herself as she poured a measure into a chipped mug and felt the warmth spread through her hands. "One luxury I don't think I could ever give up."

Tough times came and went, and Anna had met them before in her thirty years, but even she was sometimes stunned by the hardship she now saw on her own farm and on her neighbors' faces. The story had always been the same: Crop prices went up, they went down; the harvest was bountiful, the harvest was meager due to grasshoppers or hail or not enough rain. But somehow, the good usually seemed to outweigh the bad.

Not anymore. The stock market fell, taking the already low returns for crops along with it. The winters had been brutal, the summers hot and dry. First, the well pump on the windmill died, then came the heartbreaking loss of one of the calves that would have brought a fair price at market. They had their large garden, thank goodness, but it had taken hours of backbreaking work from everyone but little Lydia to keep it alive through the summer.

The basement shelves were stocked with a rainbow of fruit and vegetable jars, and the hog they butchered last month would provide much of the meat they would need until spring. Henry sometimes walked the timber with his rifle and came home with a rabbit or two. They weren't her first choice, Anna had to admit, but made into a stew they provided several meals. There was plenty of wood to keep the kitchen range and the fireplace going, even if the coal was running low. The animals were healthy, and the dairy cow was providing plenty of milk.

"We'll survive," she reminded herself as she cracked some fresh eggs into a skillet. "We always do."

"It's a cold one out there." Henry rubbed his red cheeks as he came in the kitchen door. The rumbles and thumps coming from the enclosed back porch told Anna her boys were peeling off their boots and coats. She heard a happy bark before Tippy, the family's dog, slipped around Henry and into the kitchen.

"Tippy thinks so, too." Henry had that twinkle in his blue eyes that Anna had never been able to resist. "She likes to visit, don't you, girl?"

"Please, Mother, can she stay inside today?" Horace ran into the kitchen, his woolen scarf still draped around his neck. He was always in such a hurry to get to school, and he apparently wanted to save time getting bundled up again in a few minutes. "Tippy will be great company for you while we're at school and Father's working outside."

"I've got your sister to keep me company," Anna reminded Horace as she scooped a bit of egg on a saucer to cool. Lydia was already in her wooden highchair, kicking her heels in delight as Tippy came over for a pet. But Anna couldn't say no. "I guess it will be all right. Won't it, Tippy?"

Anna loved Tippy, of course, but all the dogs she'd known as a girl had remained outside, abandoning their doghouses when winter arrived to snuggle in a straw pile in the barn.

When they got Tippy as a pup three years ago, and her tan coat and white paws inspired Henry to give her that name, she somehow knew when it was just cold enough to demand she be allowed to spend nearly all her time in the house.

Horace, in particular, had a soft spot for Tippy. He leaned over and whispered something to the dog, who wagged her tail and seemed to understand completely.

After Wilbur and Horace ran out the back porch door again, Anna stood at the double kitchen window and watched them trudge down the lane through the fresh snow, their book bundles swaying and their lunch pails bumping against the legs of their overalls.

"They'll be just fine," Henry assured her. "But if it gets any colder, I'll start up the truck and take them to school."

Anna came back to the table, determined to share a quiet cup of coffee with her husband before the work of the day really began. With the boys off at school, she could try to get ahead on the mittens she was knitting them for Christmas. There were cookies to bake, too, with just enough homemade sour cream left in the icebox to follow Henry's mother's recipe.

The laundry was piling up, but Anna hoped the weather would break and she could hang the clothes outside, rather than on the lines in the basement. If she was lucky, she might get in a few minutes of reading before supper. She'd been so tired lately, and there was so much to do ...

The coffeepot bubbled away on the kitchen range while Tippy stretched out in front of it, her paws nearly touching the stove's iron legs. Henry rose to refill his mug, then stopped.

"What is it? You're awfully quiet this morning."

"I'm just worried about Christmas." She absentmindedly rubbed the checked oilcloth that covered the wooden table by the window, and glanced out over the front pasture. It was empty this dreary morning, as Henry had decided it was too cold for the livestock to venture out.

"I know. I am, too." Henry hesitated. "But are you sure that's all that's bothering you?"

He leaned across the table and put his weathered hand over hers. Anna pulled away and reached for the half slice of toast Lydia didn't seem interested in. She chewed slowly, trying to shield her eyes from her husband's questioning gaze. Then the tears came.

"Oh, no!" Henry gasped. "Anna, please tell me. Whatever it is ..."

"I'm pregnant!" she blurted out. Her sudden wail caused Lydia to screech in her highchair, and Anna lifted the little girl into her arms. "Oh, what are we going to do?"

Henry was silent for a moment. Then he laughed. "That's wonderful! What are we going to do? Well, we'll keep doing what we've always done. Raise our family, count our blessings." Henry rushed around the table and wrapped his arms around Anna and Lydia. "And here I thought something was wrong, really wrong." He glanced at the calendar. "When? How far along are you?"

"I've only been sure for about a week. I think I'm due in June. I wanted to tell you, but I wasn't sure what you would think ..."

"Why would I be anything but thrilled? I wish you'd told me right away. No more heavy water buckets for you, my girl." Henry kissed his wife on the nose and gently wiped at her tears. "Aren't you ... aren't you happy?"

"Well, yes." Her voice wavered. "We've managed to get by this long, with God's help and us pinching every penny we can find. But how are we going to support this child? There's already five of us, and with another on the way ..."

"We'll manage somehow," Henry said soothingly, then added a spoonful of sugar to his wife's coffee cup. He knew she liked it sweet, but had been rationing everything for so long. "And the baby won't be here until next summer. That's 1933, can you imagine? Who knows, maybe we'll have a bumper crop next year and this downturn will lift. Everyone can get back on their feet then, including us."

"Oh, honey, I wish I had your positive outlook." Anna sighed. "What if things don't get better?"

"They will, someday." Henry took her hand. This time, Anna squeezed his in return. "Sooner or later. Until then, we just keep taking things one day at a time."

A big grin flashed across Henry's face. "Wait until we tell the boys, they'll be so excited."

Anna gave her husband a weary look. "You've forgotten how Wilbur resented Horace, haven't you? He was too little to understand that a baby was coming. But once Horace was here, he threw a fit."

"He got over it," Henry reminded her. "And look at them now, best friends. If anyone gets jealous this time, it'll be our little darling here." Henry took Lydia in his arms and returned to his chair. "When should we share the big news? Maybe tonight?"

Anna managed a smile. Henry always knew how to lift her spirits. "Let's wait until Christmas," she suggested. "I suppose you're right, they'll be excited. And as you know, they may not get much else for Christmas this year."

"A little brother or sister on the way could be the best gift of all." Henry sighed. "But, of course, it's not a train." He gave his wife a weary look.

"Ah, yes, the train." Anna shook her head. "Remember how they pulled that catalog out at the supper table, and they had a speech all prepared about why they needed this train and how Santa could get it for them if we didn't have enough money this year?"

Henry swallowed a gulp of his coffee, then looked down at his patched overalls. "I didn't have the heart to dash their hopes. I still don't. But it's impossible. Even if the sky rained silver dollars today, it's too late to order anything. Christmas is only a week away."

"It broke my heart, especially the part about the money." Anna sighed. "Hard work is part of growing up on a farm, and it's good for them. But these tough times are making them grow up too fast. Wilbur was up in the barn loft the other day. I thought he was playing fort, but I saw him counting the hay bales, like he was worried we might run out before next summer."

"He notices everything I do." Henry shook his head as he deposited Lydia back in her highchair. "I try to watch what I say around him, try to keep the worst of it from his ears and out of his mind. By the way, I counted those bales myself last week, and we have plenty of feed for the livestock. And straw, too. That's something to be thankful for."

"And Horace," Anna continued, "he came home the other day looking so worried. He asked me if we had lots of cardboard. Can you imagine? I said, of course we do. I guess one of the boys came to school with a hole in the sole of his boot. The boy told Miss Emmerson that he didn't have anything to cover the hole with."

Anna placed a hand over her face. That poor child ...

"Horace said the boy's sock was soaked clear through on the bottom, and it was nearly frozen to his foot. Miss Emmerson made him sit in front of the stove all morning so his feet could warm and his sock dry out. She fixed the boot, too, with something she had stored away at school."

"No one in this family will go without," Henry promised. "No matter how many of us eventually crowd around this kitchen table."

"Well, we may have to start eating all our meals in the dining room." Anna couldn't help but laugh at Henry's comment.

"Your grandmother's table is a little too fancy for my tastes, but thank goodness it has all those leaves. We'll soon need the space."

Henry leaned back in his chair, stretched his hands over his head, and looked up at the ceiling. "Now, about Christmas."

Anna laughed harder. "You have the right idea, because it's going to take many a prayer to pull this off. I've already been at it for weeks now. What do you think we can manage?"

"Well, we'll have a tree, of course. I'll take the boys down to the creek Saturday after we get back from town, and we'll pick one out. How much is in the egg money jar? Can we get a few little things, at least?"

"I counted it yesterday. If we're careful, there might be enough for some candy and a few oranges for Horace and Wilbur. But you may have to be content with those new socks I'm knitting for you."

"I'll be sure to be surprised on Christmas morning." Henry winked. "I think I can get that domino set ready for the boys. It'll take longer to paint the pieces than cut them out of the scrap wood that's in the barn. And I know you're making new mittens and hats for them and our little princess here. Now I just have to figure out what I'm going to get you."

"Don't worry about that. I don't need anything. Except a maid, to help wash these dishes. I'd better get at it, by the way, if I want to bake some bread yet this morning."

# THREE

Horace was so excited, he could barely sit still as the family's Model T truck rumbled down the frozen, rutted road toward Prosper. Last weekend, it was so icy they didn't make their usual Saturday trip to town, and his few coins were burning a hole in his coat pocket. Today's trip would be even better than usual, as it was his chance to purchase Christmas gifts along with a few pieces of candy from the glass showcase at Prosper Mercantile.

The weather had warmed at last, melting much of the earlier snow yet leaving the township's dirt roads firm enough for vehicles to pass easily, a rare stroke of luck for this time of year. Horace and Wilbur were bundled under a stack of quilts in the truck bed while Father, Mother and Lydia rode up front. Mother had gently shut down Horace's last-minute pleas to take Tippy along to town.

"But she'd love to see all the people getting ready for Christmas," he'd begged as Tippy, who'd been frolicking in the few leftover drifts of snow scattered by the back door, came over by Horace to watch the going-to-town commotion with sad eyes.

"No, she would not," Anna had admonished Horace as she placed a picnic basket to place in the truck bed. "She'd be scared. The strange horses and cars would be too much for her, and you can't take her into the stores."

Anna had paused to give Tippy a reassuring pat on the head. "We'll be back this afternoon. I will have some soup bones for her tonight. That'll be her treat."

Horace was even more discouraged when Mother insisted he wear his stocking cap with the ties that met under his chin. But now he had to admit that, as usual, Mother was right. While the day was relatively pleasant, the breeze kicked up by the truck would have chilled his ears and lifted his regular cap from his head.

Wilbur, who also wore a hat with ties, rolled his eyes. "I'm taking this off the minute we get there. I don't want any of the big town boys to see me wearing this little kids' hat. Geez."

After what seemed like hours, the storage tower of Prosper's feed store appeared on the eastern horizon. Horace always marveled at its height, as the wooden structure had to be at least twice as tall as his house. The idea of the zillions of bushels of corn and oats inside, stored away for months, fascinated him.

Nearly a dozen farm wagons crowded the feed store's parking lot, with a few trucks thrown in for good measure. While the Schermanns didn't need to make any purchases there today, Horace knew his father would head to the feed store to catch up on the news as soon as he'd dropped everyone else on Main Street.

"Look at all those people." Wilbur pointed as the truck rumbled into the main part of town. "I think everyone in the county is here today."

Henry squeezed the truck into a space by Prosper Savings Bank, and both boys gasped. A string of colored electric lights glowed inside the plate-glass window.

"I wish we had those at home." Horace could hardly breathe. "Wouldn't those look great on our tree?"

"They sure would." Wilbur crawled over to Horace's side to get a better look. "Someday, we'll get electricity at the farm and we'll have our tree crammed full of those lights. Wait and see."

While Horace pondered that possibility, Anna got out of the cab with Lydia in her arms.

"Now, boys." She gave them each a look. "I expect you to behave yourselves. Us girls are going over to the millinery shop. I can't afford to buy anything, but it will be fun to see all the new fabrics and hats."

Seeing the blank looks on her sons' faces, Anna changed the subject. "Never mind. You can go to the drug store across the street if you want, then down to Prosper Mercantile. Your father's going to the feed store, but we will all meet at the mercantile at noon."

As the boys clambered out of the back of the truck, Henry leaned out the window. "Wilbur, do you have your pocket watch? Good. When Mother says noon, she means noon."

Henry reached into his coat pocket and pulled out two dimes, which brought big grins to his sons' faces.

"Get yourselves some candy, and something for Mother for Christmas."

Horace and Wilbur were suddenly on their own, free as could be for nearly two hours. All around them, car horns tooted, horses stomped their hooves, and people called to friends and laughed as they juggled their paper-wrapped packages. It was almost overwhelming.

"Where to first?" Wilbur clutched his dime in his fist. "With that quarter I had saved back, I'm practically a millionaire."

Horace, who kept his coins in a tiny tin box behind the dresser in their bedroom, had even more to spend. A whole forty cents!

"I smell popcorn. Look! Over there, in front of the movie house." A man with a small cart handed out paper bags to a group of children. "Let's go there first!"

The boys munched their popcorn as they strolled down Main Street. They eyed the candy display at the drug store, but decided to wait. The bigger selection was at Prosper Mercantile, after all. But they used some of their coins to buy a set of handkerchiefs for Mother.

Next was a stop at the library. Horace didn't have a patrons' card, and they lived too far from town for one to be useful, anyway. But he loved the library, with its quiet aisles, orderly shelves and thick carpet. Someday, when he was grown up and had lots of money, he'd have all kinds of books. Father and Mother loved to read, and the shelves beside the fireplace were well-stocked, but Horace dreamed of having his own collection.

The librarian let Wilbur and Horace wander around for a bit, then motioned them to a back corner. "We have cookies today, a special treat because it's nearly Christmas."

Horace's eyes grew wide at the assortment of sweets on the tray. He gave Wilbur a questioning look.

"Mother would be mad," Wilbur said finally. "She'd say we ruined our appetites for lunch. But hey, we've already had popcorn. Might as well."

"Put them in your pockets if you like," the librarian said with a twinkle in her eye as each boy reached for a cookie. "Save them for later."

There was a gathering of children in front of Prosper Mercantile, whose green awnings sheltered two expansive windows filled with toys. It was the biggest store in town, an impressive space filled with housewares, clothing, and anything else anyone could ever need. Around back, there was a lumberyard where men could pull up their trucks and wagons and load supplies through what had to be the largest set of doors Horace had ever seen.

Wilbur gave the front door's handle a tug. "Let's see what they have for Father and Mother and Lydia." The jingling bell above announced their arrival, and it took the boys a moment to get their bearings. The store was bright and crowded, with dazzling electric lights dangling from a high ceiling coated in decorative tin.

Horace took a deep breath, and enjoyed the sweet aroma drifting from a wooden crate of oranges by the cash register and the unmistakable scent of nuts tucked in the bins along the far wall. Men gathered around the potbellied stove, swapping stories while their wives shopped. Wilbur and Horace first found a blue-striped tie for Father. He'd only wear it to church, but it was nice and fit their budget. They chose some embroidered handkerchiefs for Mother, and a small rattle for Lydia.

Then it was time to approach the oak counter that ran down the middle of the store. It was massive, and at this time of year was always draped with ropes of greenery tied with red velvet bows.

The display case was beautiful, but that wasn't what inspired awe in the boys.

It was the glowing jewels of candy just behind the glass, where small wooden cubes overflowed with a rainbow of flavors and colors. Mr. Shrader, who owned the store, was behind the counter as usual, a spotless white apron tied around his middle.

"What can I get you boys today?" Mr. Shrader glanced their way over the glasses perched on his nose and offered his usual hearty smile. He already knew the answer to his question. Every penny counted. Big decisions had to be made.

"We're just looking for now, Mr. Shrader," Wilbur said as Horace, suddenly speechless, pressed his face to the glass.

"You take your time." Mr. Shrader stifled a laugh. "I'll ring up these other customers first, then help you when you're ready."

As the boys eyed the dizzying array of candy options, Wilbur couldn't help but glance toward the front windows. There were toy trucks in the boys' display, baseball gloves and, yes, even a train.

Wilbur saw it right away when they crossed the street, but had done his best to keep Horace from discovering it. And now, Wilbur told himself he wasn't going to even look at that train. Besides, nothing would measure up to the set they found in the catalog. That was a far superior train to anything that could be found in a small-town shop window. He was sure of it.

Trying to distract himself, Wilbur turned his gaze toward the girls' window. Suddenly, he grabbed Horace by the arm. "Hey, let's go look over there."

"At girls' stuff?" Horace grimaced and pulled away. "Whatever for?"

"I see a small doll over there. What say we get it for Lydia?"

In the end, he convinced Horace to upgrade Lydia's gift. The doll cost more, meaning less money for candy, but Wilbur was right.

"She's too young for candy, so we can't share our stash with her," he reminded Horace. "And soon, she won't be a baby anymore. She'll need toys, and she won't want ours."

The boys were waiting out front when Father returned. He covered his eyes while Horace and Wilbur hid their packages in an empty flour sack in the truck bed. Anna and Lydia soon joined them and, after they ate their sandwiches, the boys watched their sister while Anna and Henry went back into Prosper Mercantile to stretch their money as far as they could.

The bags of flour, sugar and coffee went in the back of the truck, but Anna kept a smaller sack close and wouldn't let the boys look inside.

After the bumpy ride home, it was time to unpack the truck and warm themselves in the kitchen. Henry, Wilbur and Horace took the boys' sled to the creek and selected a tree.

The ornate iron stand came out of storage upstairs, and Anna set up the boys with paper and flour paste at the dining-room table so they could create chains to drape around the tree. Henry trimmed a few branches to make the tree more symmetrical, and Anna arranged the extra bits of greenery on top of the dining room's built-in buffet and around the mantel clock above the fireplace. The bracing scent of evergreen soon filled the farmhouse.

Once the tree was settled in the stand and festooned with paper chains and the family's homemade ornaments, Anna brought out a varnished wooden box. Inside, wrapped in sheets of tissue paper wrinkled with the passing of years, rested a set of amber glass ball ornaments that told of a more prosperous time. There was also a silver-plated tree topper, and a set of red glass cardinals.

"Would you like to do the honors this year, Mr. Schermann?" Anna teased Henry. He had bought the cardinals for their first Christmas as a couple, ten years ago.

"I would be glad to, Mrs. Schermann." Henry carefully took the glass birds from his wife's hands and looped them, side by side, at the top of the tree.

Anna took a step back and smiled. The tree was beautiful, as always, and the pair of cardinals yet another reminder of the love she had for Henry and their children. There were dishes to wash and supper to prepare, but for a moment, she was content to glance around her cozy home and offer a quick, silent prayer of gratitude.

"I think we've outdone ourselves once again." She turned to Henry and gave him a quick kiss. "Maybe we'll have a wonderful Christmas, after all."

# FOUR

It was Tuesday afternoon, just three days until Christmas, when the crank telephone sounded in the kitchen. Anna was down in the cellar and rushed up the stairs, her heart pounding. The telephone so rarely rang, and she feared the worst.

"Hello?" Anna tried to steady her voice. "Oh, yes, John, how are you?" John Leary and his wife, Lottie, lived a mile south of the Schermanns. They were elderly, and Anna often wondered how much longer they could continue to live on their own.

"Oh, I'm sorry to hear that. The poor horse. Yes, I'm sure Henry can come over to help you. He's out in the barn. I'll ring you back right away."

Anna bundled up and stepped out into the farmyard. It had turned colder again, and the air was damp. She slid the latch on the barn door and was met by Tippy, as well as a chorus of greetings from the cows and sheep. Ted and Bertha, the family's horses, were in their stalls at the far end of the barn, and Anna took a moment to cuddle one of the barn cats who sauntered down the aisle in her direction.

"Henry?" Anna called over the banging noises coming from inside the grain room. The door was barely ajar, and she took a step back. Perhaps he was up to something, and she didn't want to ruin a surprise. It was nearly Christmas, after all.

The noise stopped. "Wait. Don't come in!" Henry peeked around the door with a mischievous grin. His smile faded when he saw the concern on Anna's face.

"John Leary just telephoned. King caught his foot in a fence. John doesn't think he broke his leg, but he's limping. He's hoping you can come over and give him a hand."

"Sure thing." Henry ducked back inside the grain room. "Can you please ring him back? I'll head over right away."

Henry was relieved the temperamental Model T started in such damp air. He serviced the old truck as best as he could, but it had been some time since there'd been any money to replace parts or even think about trading it in for a newer model. When the truck refused to run, he always had the option of hitching Bertha and Ted to the farm wagon, but the truck was so much faster. And John needed his help this afternoon.

The Schermanns may have been barely scraping along, but the Learys were far-more destitute. Both John and Lottie were nearly eighty, and had no close family nearby. Their son didn't live past twenty, dying from some disease Henry couldn't now recall. The daughter had been a real beauty, everyone always said so, but she'd run off to Chicago with a railroad man when she was still a teenager and rarely visited.

The elderly couple's house was very old, and hidden in a grove of trees at the end of a long lane. Henry was sure it was one of the first frame dwellings built in Fulton Township. The Learys hadn't raised cash crops for a few years, and now relied only on their garden and a few livestock.

Henry had always liked John and Lottie, and continued to give them a hand when needed, just as his father and mother had done for decades. He wasn't about to let John try to corner an injured horse on his own.

Lottie, with a tattered shawl around her slight shoulders, waved from the door of their steep-roofed house when Henry bumped into the yard. She gestured for him to head for the barn. The paint on the house was so faded, Henry wasn't sure what color it had been at one time. John's truck, which was parked under a bare-limbed tree, was in even worse shape than Henry's Model T.

John was waiting just inside the barn door with a basin of water and a spotless pile of rags.

"Sorry to be trouble." John offered Henry a feeble handshake. Henry knew his neighbor was nearly bald under his woolen cap, but the old man took pride in keeping his white beard neat. "But King's got a gash on his front left there. I got Lady tied up so she's not in the way. Then I decided to wait for you."

"I'm glad you did." Henry opened the wooden gate, then reached for the basin and cloths John handed over the fence before he joined Henry on the other side. "It doesn't look too bad. Let's get him fixed up."

King wasn't too pleased with all the unusual attention, but the men soon had the wound washed and covered. Henry wrapped the horse's leg in a makeshift splint and promised John he'd come over after Christmas to give it another look. John insisted Henry stop in the house for a cup of coffee before he started for home, and Henry welcomed the chance for a neighborly visit. Work around the farm slowed this time of year, but the unpredictable weather and bad roads meant it could be weeks before the Schermanns made it farther than the little Lutheran church just down the road.

Lottie was also eager for company, and had set out a plate of oatmeal cookies on what had to be her best tablecloth. The house was spotless, but Henry's heart ached to see the meager stack of wood by the cook stove and the rags stuffed in the bottoms of the window frames. Before he headed for home, he insisted on helping John carry in more wood from the shed behind the house.

Henry knew better than to ask John if he was stocked up on coal. Every year, once the calendar flipped over to November, the elderly couple closed off all their rooms except the kitchen and the parlor, where they had moved their bed years ago when they could no longer get up the steep, narrow steps to the two tiny rooms above.

John chattered about this and that as he walked Henry out to the Model T. But as Henry opened the truck door, John laid a tentative hand on his arm.

"Now Henry, I know you don't want my money," John started in a halting voice.

"You're right about that," Henry said gently.

John pulled some coins from his pocket. "You've always been so good to us, and so were your parents. It's been a rare occasion that you've allowed me to pay up my account, so to speak. But it's a cold day, and I couldn't fix King's leg on my own. This is a fraction of what I would've paid Doc Kinley over in Prosper, and it would have taken him at least a day to get out this far."

Henry pushed his friends' thin fingers back over the coins. "Merry Christmas, John. I was glad to help. You save that money for some time when you really need it."

※ ※ ※

Anna was watching out the kitchen windows when the truck rumbled up the drive. It got dark so early these days, and she was glad to see Henry home safe.

"The boys have already started chores. How's King?" Anna stepped away from the stove long enough to give Henry a kiss. She was frying pieces of leftover pork chops with a large quantity of potatoes, onions and carrots, stretching the meal as far as she could.

"King's pride is hurt worse than his leg. He'll pull through just fine. Anna, I have an idea. What do you say to us asking John and Lottie over for Christmas dinner?"

Anna smiled as she reached for a pinch of salt. "I'd love that. I hate to think of them being over there all alone. That daughter of theirs never seems to make it back," she added with a scowl. "But you know, we've tried that before with no success. John and Lottie are too proud. If they think we're asking them out of pity, they'll kindly decline."

"You're right. But if we insist they bring something, they might say yes this time. John offered me money again, of course, but ..."

"You wouldn't accept it, I know." Anna smiled at her husband. "We'll never take a cent from those wonderful people. They remind me of my grandparents, God rest their souls. I'd be honored to have them here for Christmas dinner. Tell you what. After supper, I'll ring over and see if I can persuade them to join us."

She was thrilled when John, after much fussing and consulting with Lottie, accepted their invitation.

"They are bringing two pumpkin pies," she told Henry after she rang off from the party line. "Oh, is this going to be fun!" It touched Henry to see the excited smile on his wife's face, a smile that had been absent lately.

"Let's see ... we don't have a turkey, but I've got a ham, and plenty of potatoes and carrots." Anna ticked items off on her fingers. "There are canned green beans in the cellar. We're blessed to have so many bins of apples down there, so I can still make the stuffing, even though I don't have any raisins and the price was just too dear at Prosper Mercantile the other day. There'll be rolls, and plum jam to spread on them."

She moved into the dining room and rummaged through the built-in buffet's drawers. "Where is that red-and-white tablecloth? Not the plaid, but the one with the flowers on it. Yes, here it is."

"I'm sorry that we had to trade the wedding china for that load of oats three years ago." Henry sighed and wrapped his arms around his wife. "I hated to do it, but our crop was so small and ..."

"Oh, never mind that." Anna shrugged. "It was beautiful, to be sure, but we never used it. Better that the livestock had something to eat than letting those dishes gather dust. I have just enough plates to go around, I think. We'll manage."

"What's going on?" Wilbur was doing his homework at the dining room table by the light of a kerosene lantern. Horace, who had been reading one of the mystery magazines by the fireplace, came through the archway to see what the commotion was about.

"Boys, we're having company for Christmas!" Anna all but sang out the words. "And not like the times Grandpa and Grandma or other family come to visit. I mean true company. You know John and Lottie Leary, just south of here? They're having dinner with us."

Horace felt his stomach drop. John was a good friend of Father's, and Lottie liked to ruffle his hair and give him cookies, but he sometimes felt shy around people he didn't know well.

And there would be plenty of socializing in the coming days. Grandma and Grandpa Schermann's celebration was Saturday, then Mother's whole family was coming to the farm Sunday. It was a major event that meant hours of scrubbing and fussing when Horace would rather be reading a book. Wouldn't it be nicer to just have the house to themselves on Christmas, to not entertain guests? Would this mean he had to set aside his overalls and wear his church clothes all day?

Anna frowned. "Horace, what's wrong?"

"I don't know," he mumbled. "I guess they can come over. I guess maybe it will make Christmas more special this year, especially if Santa can't come."

The room fell silent. Horace instantly wished he could take his words back, swallow them somehow.

Father sighed. Wilbur quickly looked down at his schoolwork. Tippy, who had wedged herself under the Christmas tree, offered Horace a kind look and a sympathetic thump of her tail. Was Mother starting to cry?

"Santa won't forget you this Christmas, Horace." Anna quickly crossed the room and put her arms around her youngest son. "Santa never forgets. You've been a good boy this year." She turned to include Wilbur in her gaze. "Both of you have."

Wilbur picked at the clasp of one overall buckle and wouldn't look at his mother. "Yeah, we've tried to be good." He sighed. "But there's not going to be a train, is there?"

Henry's mouth set in a firm line. Anna shook her head at him and looked away.

"Sometimes, Santa can't bring us everything we want." Henry knelt by Wilbur's chair. "Life is like that too, boys, things don't always go your way. Lydia is too small to understand, but you are big enough now to see that, to see what's been going on around this farm the past how-many years. Your mother and I are doing all we can, and you've been such a big help." At this, Wilbur sat up straighter. "We have food to eat, and feed for the animals, and we have each other."

"There's not much coal in the cellar." Horace began to cry. "Mother, when I saw you looking at it the other day, you didn't tell me everything was all right. Why didn't you tell me it's all going to be all right?"

"Oh, my dear." Anna pulled him close. "I'm so sorry. It will be. We just have to be careful to not use too much coal, that's all. Let's poke around for some more blankets for your boys' bed. How does that sound?" Horace hesitated, then nodded.

"And we've got rows of trees out there in the windbreak," Henry said cheerfully as he tried to push down his feelings. It was one thing to worry over every expense, but it broke his heart to see the fear in his boys' eyes. "There's plenty of wood for the stove and the fireplace. And I have two strong boys to help me chop it, don't I?"

Wilbur tried for a smile. Horace could only nod again.

"For now, let's just look forward to Christmas." Anna rubbed her hands in expectation. "Santa will come, and your Father and I have some surprises in store. Tomorrow is the party at school, then you don't have to go back for over a week!" This made Wilbur and Horace brighten. "We'll go to church Christmas Eve, open presents in the morning, and then John and Lottie will visit. We don't need lots of money or mounds of presents to have a good Christmas, right?"

Horace started to feel a little better. "Can we have corn relish for Christmas dinner?" The pungent mix of vegetables was his favorite recipe the family canned every year. Most people thought a little corn relish went a long way, but Horace would eat as much as Mother would let him.

Anna laughed. "Yes, Horace, I think we can manage that. Now, let's get ready for bed."

# FIVE

The program at school was a success. Horace quickly lost his stage fright once he spotted Mother and Father in the crowd, and delivered his lines without a hitch. Wilbur starred as one of the Wise Men in the Nativity scene, and then it was time for punch and cookies.

Suddenly, there was a hearty "Ho, ho, ho!" in the cloak room and Santa burst in. His velvet suit was a little threadbare and the pack he carried wasn't very large, but the children were still thrilled with the small sticks of candy he passed around.

One of the older boys, however, was skeptical. "I didn't see any reindeer out front."

"Santa sometimes travels in a truck these days," Wilbur shot back, hoping Horace hadn't heard the other boy's comment. "The reindeer need to rest up for Christmas Eve, and you know that's tomorrow night."

Horace and Wilbur helped Father in the barn the next morning, spreading fresh straw for the animals and bringing down more hay from the loft.

Just before noon, the sunshine faded over the bare, rolling fields.

"Let's bring more wood into the back porch," Father said. "I smell snow."

"How do you do that?" Horace turned this way and that in the farmyard, filling his chest with each breath.

Father laughed. "It's just an expression. I can't smell it, really. But I can sort of feel it. There's a dampness in the air. It's getting colder. Might as well get ready."

By late afternoon, a few snowflakes were spotted out the kitchen windows. More were drifting down when it was time for evening chores. After they finished tending to the livestock, Father took a metal bin out of the barn's grain room and filled it with fresh hay, then set it outside the barn door.

An old superstition claimed that hay blanketed with Christmas morning's frost was special, that it protected the animals through the coming year. Henry knew it had to be just a tall tale, but it comforted him to continue the tradition his father and grandfather had taught him.

"Does this really work?" Wilbur eyed the bin. "There's not much in there, it's not like any one animal gets more than a mouthful."

"You're right," Henry admitted. "But I guess it's enough to do the trick. I'll take all the help I can get these days. Let's get inside, now. Mother has soup on the stove and we need to get to church."

\* \* \*

Horace tried not to fidget during services. The sermon seemed so long, and the bare wooden pew was hard, but at least the hymns gave him a chance to stand and stretch. The altar in their little country church was draped with a few evergreen boughs, and red bows graced the railing of the platform where the piano stood.

Father had quietly informed the boys there would be no small paper sacks of nuts and candy this year, as the church board couldn't afford the annual tradition. Horace had been disappointed, but his resignation turned to awe when he saw the towering Christmas tree.

It was adorned with dozens of tiny white candles, whose flames flickered in the drafts that seeped in around the church's windows. Two men stood watch with buckets, ready to flood the tree in case the candles' heat leaped to one of the branches.

While their tree at home was lovely, with its tin-foil squares, painted nutshells and delicate glass ornaments, Father and Mother never allowed candles on it. The scorch mark on the dining room's oak floor was a grim reminder of one year when Father was a child. A candle had wobbled loose from its branch and nearly set the tree on fire.

The peacefulness of the service and the smiles on his neighbors' faces raised Horace's spirits. He remembered the family's conversation from the other night, how Mother and Father had assured him everything would be fine.

The space beneath their Christmas tree was rarely empty; Tippy had seen to that. But oh, how wonderful it would be if there would be a train under there in the morning, a real tin train with shiny paint and a circle track. He and Wilbur could load its cars with pebbles, or shelled corn, or twigs standing in for loads of lumber. They could pretend to be real farmers like Father, taking their crops to market. Maybe robbers would hijack the train. The conductor would be brave, and save the day by reaching for his pistol ...

Surely it couldn't hurt, Horace decided, to ask God one more time. His Sunday school teacher said when the children prayed in church, they should close their eyes and think about the cross above the altar. Horace looked at it now, but wasn't sure it fit this specific prayer. Wasn't it more useful for thanking God for His blessings, for asking Him to protect your family, things like that?

Horace then eyed the Baby Jesus, sleeping in His manger by the pastor's pulpit, and hesitated once more. Baby Jesus was so tiny, could He really make this happen? Besides, Horace knew it was just a doll.

Then he turned his gaze again to the Christmas tree, to the warm glow that spread out from its branches like dozens of tiny halos. The tree was magnificent, it dominated the room on this holy night. Horace squeezed his eyes shut, and gave it his all.

The snow began to fall more steadily during services, and the wind was swirling in from the northwest by the time they reached home. Father backed the truck into the shed, then made a quick trip to the barn to check the livestock before joining the rest of the family by the fireplace. Mother brought out a tin of sugared walnuts

Father had cracked out while the boys were at school, and the caramel corn she made that afternoon.

By bedtime, the flakes had drifted thick on the ground, and the wind howled around the corners of the farmhouse and rumbled in the chimney. After much debate between Horace and Wilbur, the reindeers' carrots were left on Santa's cookie plate by the fireplace rather than on the back porch steps. Horace decided Santa might fall behind schedule because of the snowstorm and not have time to race around to the back of the house.

"I prayed for us to get the train," Horace whispered to Wilbur as they huddled under the bedcovers, Tippy curled up on her own blanket at the foot of the bed.

"I suppose it couldn't hurt." Wilbur sighed as he pulled the quilts closer to his nose. "It's like Father, putting out that hay. Who knows if it'll do any good? But listen to that storm. Santa's got a tough trip tonight. We shouldn't get our hopes up."

"I know," Horace mumbled. "But if anyone can bring us our train, it has to be Santa."

# SIX

The blizzard had blown itself out by dawn, and the snow glittered in the first sunbeams that appeared over the eastern horizon.

Everything was coated with a thick blanket of snow; the bare tree branches and the fence lines looked as if they'd been dipped in frosting overnight.

Etchings of ice covered the farmhouse's windowpanes, reflecting the light of the kerosene lamp as Horace and Wilbur hurriedly dressed for the day. Mother had come to their door to wish them "Merry Christmas" and to give them good news: They could wear their usual overalls and thick flannel shirts all day, even after chores. No dress clothes would be required.

"I just hope John and Lottie can still come," Anna said in a low voice to Henry as he started the coffeepot on the back of the kitchen range. "It's a beautiful day, but that snow looks deep."

"Their truck is even older than ours," Henry admitted.

"And I don't know if I should try to get ours going and head over there and pick them up."

"No, no, we can't risk that." Anna shook her head as she checked on the pan of cinnamon rolls in the oven. "What if you got stuck in a drift? I don't know which would be worse, if you were all alone or had those sweet elderly people with you. Let's see if they call this morning, what they say."

She paused, and leaned toward the dining room. "Here come the boys."

Horace's heart thumped in his chest as he and Wilbur rounded the stairwell's bend with Tippy at their heels.

Would the train be there? Did his hasty prayer last night, however self-absorbed, trigger some sort of Christmas miracle?

"Merry Christmas!" Henry and Anna shouted as the boys came into the dining room. There were several small packages under the tree, including one marked To Wilbur and Horace, from Santa.

But no train. Horace's heart sank. He couldn't look at Wilbur, not sure if it would be worse to see disappointment or a bitter, smug look on his brother's face. And he couldn't bear to see Mother cry as she had the other night, so he managed a smile and ran with Wilbur to study the packages.

Christmas, Horace knew, was about more than getting gifts. He had to make the best of it. At least Santa had come; there was that one special parcel under the tree, after all, and only crumbs remained on the plate by the fireplace.

"Let's hand out the presents in the sitting room," Mother suggested as she passed around the cinnamon rolls. The sight of their creamy icing raised Horace's spirits. "Then we'll eat after chores."

The package from Santa contained a magnificent set of black dominoes with yellow dots. What a racket they made when they toppled each other on the hardwood floor! They must have really been from Santa, Horace decided, because Mother would have said they made too much noise.

He got a new knit cap in a rich shade of navy, one with a brim on the front like the older boys wore. It even had a fold-down flap to cover his ears and the back of his neck, and mittens to match. Horace continued to marvel over how Mother could create such fine things with just a few knitting needles and dyed yarn spun from the wool of their sheep.

There were socks, too, and nuts and candy and oranges from Prosper Mercantile. Father exclaimed over his tie, and Mother gave them each a kiss after she found the delicate embroidered handkerchiefs in her package. Lydia squealed with delight over her doll, and Horace saw Mother wipe away tears as he and Wilbur told how they had sacrificed some of their candy money to get their sister a gift.

Father mumbled about needing to check something outside, then disappeared. He appeared again in the kitchen doorway, carrying the family's baby cradle. But it looked different.

"Oh, Henry!" Anna leaped from her rocking chair and embraced her husband. "It looks beautiful! The soft green color is perfect!"

"Well, I decided if we were going to need it again, it was time to fix those broken spindles." Henry grinned. "Then I thought it needed a fresh coat of paint. I searched in the cellar to see what we had around. It was this green, or black or yellow, so ..."

Henry and Anna turned to see the surprise and confusion on their sons' faces.

"Well, boys, we have an announcement to make." Anna clapped her hands. "You're getting a new little brother or sister in the summer! Isn't that wonderful?"

"Wowza!" Wilbur shouted. "I hope it's a boy! Horace, wouldn't that be great? We'll be able to play real baseball. One to pitch, one to hit, one to field ..."

"Maybe it'll be a girl, instead!" Horace exclaimed. "Then we'll be two girls and two boys, half of each!"

"We'll cross that bridge when we come to it." Father gave Mother a quick kiss. "For now, let's get those chores done."

Horace was actually happy to shovel the back steps that morning. The farm looked like a fairyland dusted with the new snow, like a picture out of a storybook. Father shoveled a path to the barn, then shook the heavy snow off the hay in the metal tin and let Horace and Wilbur feed it to the horses, sheep and cows, one handful at a time. Horace poured out a saucer of cream and some meat scraps for the three barn cats, and then helped Wilbur and Father toss chunks of carrots into the other animals' troughs.

"Everyone gets a little something extra for Christmas," Father reminded the boys as they set out the rest of the feed. "Remember the Christmas story? The animals in the stable played a very important role. Next to Mary and Joseph, they were the first to see Baby Jesus. Horace, do you have those treats for the chickens?"

"Yes, Father." He handed the cats' cream can to Wilbur and ran for the barn door. "I'll get over there right away. I don't need a shovel!"

What fun it was to plunge through the snow, white puffs flying as his boots made deep craters in the drifts! In some places, the piles were as high as Horace's knees; in other spots between the barn and the chicken house, the snow was only a few inches deep. The full brunt of winter was still to come; by February, lugging a water pail on this chilly trip to the chickens wouldn't be fun anymore. But today ...

Horace scraped the snow away from the bottom of the coop door with his mittened hand and opened it to a chorus of clucks and squawks. He emptied and refilled their water pans, scooped feed from the wooden box in the corner, and then set out the chunks of pumpkin and the sunflower seeds. Horace latched the chicken coop door behind him and started for the house, making more tracks in the fresh snow and looking forward to the hearty breakfast that waited in the kitchen.

Anna considered her options after the dishes were cleared, then started a pumpkin pie. Surely John and Lottie wouldn't make it over for dinner, and maybe it was for the best. The Learys had each other, as they'd had for more than fifty years, and at least they were safe and sound at home.

If the roads improved tomorrow, she would have Henry head over with some leftovers. Her family would adapt, as they always did, go on with their celebration and thank God for the many blessings in their lives. Anna instinctively patted her stomach and smiled.

She was coming up the cellar stairs with a basket of food jars and potatoes when she heard a strange sound. Was that a bell?

She paused on the landing, listening. It wasn't in the house. Was it coming from outside?

"Someone's here!" Wilbur shouted from the dining room. "Look, Horace, they've got a big sled!"

Anna set the basket on the kitchen sideboard and hurried to the windows just as Henry ran in from where he'd been reading a newspaper by the fireplace.

"Would you look at that? It's John and Lottie!" Henry reached for his coat. The merry music of bells rang out again as the red sleigh, pulled by Lady, glided up the driveway and eased to a stop by the back porch steps.

Henry reached the sleigh just in time for Lottie to hand him a large round cake safe, telling him to be careful because her pies were stacked inside. Once she stepped to the ground, Lottie retrieved her package and started for the door.

"John, I can't believe it!" Henry hurried around the sleigh to give his neighbor a hearty handshake. "We were just about to ring you up. Anna and I figured the roads were too bad for your truck to get through." He stepped back and gave a low whistle. "This is some sleigh. I didn't even know you had this."

"It's been tucked away in the back of the barn for too long." John chuckled. "When it started to snow yesterday afternoon, we decided it wasn't safe to set out for church, at our age. We feared we couldn't come today, either. Lottie was so disappointed, and so was I. Then, I had an idea."

He gave the sleigh's side a reverent pat. "I went out to the barn and dusted this thing off. King is doing well, thanks to you, but he's still a little grumpy and not his usual good company for Lady. I figured a dash through the snow might cheer her up, and it sure has." As if in answer, Lady proudly tossed her head and shook her sleigh bells.

"Back in the day, this was the only way to get around this time of year," John continued. "I figured, why not? I've seen almost eighty Christmases, and you never know what the future might bring. I decided we weren't going to let an invitation like this pass us by."

"I'm so glad you didn't." Henry clapped his friend on the shoulder. "Let's get Lady unhitched and settled in the barn, then get inside by the fire."

As the two men returned to the sleigh and prepared to spread an old lap robe over its faded brocade cushions, Henry noticed a wooden box tucked behind the seat.

John watched his friend's face closely, then answered Henry's questioning look with his own grin. "Looks like I forgot something. Why don't you have Horace and Wilbur come help me get that crate into the house?"

Horace and Wilbur were already on the back porch, pulling on their boots and coats. They'd seen pictures of sleighs in books and magazines. But they'd never been able to inspect one, admire its swooping lines and curved iron runners.

"I could use your help," John told the boys. "See if you can get that box for me. Your father and I will hold the door."

"What do you think's in here?" Horace whispered to Wilbur as they moved sideways toward the steps, careful of the box they carried between them.

"Don't know." Wilbur frowned, thinking it over. "It's kind of heavy, but not really. How many pies was Lottie supposed to bring, anyway?"

"Let's set it on the kitchen table," Lottie suggested as the boys carried in the crate. John unhooked the latch and lifted the lid.

"A train!" Horace shouted so loudly that Tippy began to bark and rushed in from the dining room. "It's a train! It worked! It worked!"

The kitchen erupted in rounds of shouts and cheers. Except for Wilbur, who was frozen, speechless, as his eyes took in the ornate golden scrollwork on the sides of the black tin engine, the calligraphy lettering on the four freight cars, and the tiny cutout windows in the passenger car. There was a yellow caboose, complete with a back door and railing, and curves of metal track resting in the bottom of the crate.

The cars were different colors, red and blue and green. Just like the ad in the catalog had promised. But this wasn't the same train. It was far better, more luxurious, and even finer than the set Wilbur had spied in the window at Prosper Mercantile.

Henry could hardly speak. "What ... how ... where did you get this?"

"Did you tell them the boys wanted a train?" Anna asked him, crying tears of joy. She wiped her face with her apron while Lottie wrapped a warm arm around her shoulder.

"No, I swear I didn't." Henry just shook his head and turned to John, who watched Horace and Wilbur with a mixture of delight and sadness on his lined face. "How did you know? I can't even ..."

"All young boys love trains," John said quietly. "Ours did, too."

Horace and Wilbur paused in their exclamations and turned to see a few tears in John's eyes. Horace rushed over and threw his arms around his neighbor's waist, Wilbur right behind.

"Thank you, Mr. Leary," Horace gasped. He still couldn't believe it. It really was a Christmas miracle! "I wished for a train so bad, we both did. Last night at church, I even said a special prayer that we would get it. And we did!"

"But not how we thought we would," Wilbur added. "It's the best gift ever! I told Horace that we couldn't get disappointed if it didn't happen."

"On Christmas Day, all little boys' dreams should come true." Lottie squeezed John's hand. "Horace and Wilbur, why don't you get that train set up around the tree. It's been decades since I've seen it in action." The boys rushed off with the crate, Tippy right behind.

"I don't know what to say." Henry rubbed his hands together. "John, Lottie, it's too much. Don't you want to keep it? It must mean so much to you."

"It's never too much trouble to show friends that you care," John replied. "Henry and Anna, you've been there for us time and again. And I know how you feel about taking any money," he gently scolded Henry, who could only laugh.

"Our Robert loved that train," Lottie added. "We'd had an especially good harvest that year, got a little ahead for once. He saw it in a catalog, wanted it so badly. We wrote away for it, picked it up at the depot over in Prosper in that very box. He grew up, of course, and the train was packed away."

Lottie paused for a moment and her voice grew softer. "And then when he died, without having any children of his own ... we couldn't bear to get it out again, and we couldn't bear to give it away."

John nodded. "After you helped me with King the other day, we talked it over. We wondered how we could thank you. It was tough to get that crate out, to see the train again. But it was in great shape, only a bit dusty. We decided then and there it was time to let it go."

Lottie smiled as Horace and Wilbur's excited shouts echoed from the dining room. "Trains are meant to be played with, to be enjoyed. It wasn't right, leaving it in that crate when there were two wonderful little boys right under our noses. John didn't recall ever seeing a toy train here. We know times are hard for everyone. We took a chance that this would be the perfect gift."

Anna gave each of her neighbors a hug. "We agonized over this for weeks, prayed for guidance. The money just wasn't there. We can't put our gratitude into words."

"What does everyone say? 'The Lord works in mysterious ways.'" Lottie raised an eyebrow. "Anna, how about I help you get dinner ready while you big boys get in there and show Horace and Wilbur how it's done?"

Henry stood back a bit, shaking his head and smiling, to give John room to crouch next to Horace and Wilbur under the tree. Horace could hardly believe the excitement on his elderly neighbor's face as John showed the boys how to latch the track into a circle, and the right way to hitch the cars so they wouldn't bang together as they rounded a bend.

John Leary's blue eyes twinkled, and his hearty laugh rang through the house. Horace noticed his neighbor's white beard, and then the red wool cap that, in all the excitement, John had forgotten to remove when he came into the house.

Horace suddenly remembered how Mother and Father said Santa was everywhere, all the time. Maybe they were right.

# RECIPES

## Caramel Corn

This is perfect for holiday gifts. My mom got this recipe from a neighbor, added the peanuts and makes it every year with her old electric air popper. If you want it less sweet, use more popcorn. After the caramel corn is baked and cooled, eat as-is or stir in other goodies, like M&Ms, craisins, whatever!

Put in a large kettle on the stove:
2 sticks margarine (1 cup)
1/2 cup white corn syrup
2 cups brown sugar
Bring to a boil, then turn down and cook for 5 minutes, keep watching it and stirring it so it doesn't burn.

Remove the sugar mixture from the heat and add 1/2 teaspoon of baking soda. Stir well.

On large cookie sheets or in oven-safe pans, mix: 8 quarts of popped popcorn (plain) with salted peanuts (2 or 3 eight-ounce bags is about right). Pour the sugar mixture over the nuts and popcorn, and stir. Bake for one hour at 225 degrees, stirring every 15 minutes.

\* \* \*

**Apple Raisin Dressing**
My maternal grandmother often made this for Thanksgiving and Christmas, and our family holidays aren't complete without it. It's the perfect mix of savory with a little sweet. This recipe is easy to double for a crowd.

Place in a large bowl:
14 slices of dry bread, broken into smaller pieces
3 large apples, peeled, cored, cut into smaller pieces
1/2 cup raisins
1/2 teaspoon cinnamon
1/4 teaspoon allspice
1/4 teaspoon nutmeg
1/4 cup sugar
salt and pepper to taste

Mix these together and stir into the bread mixture:
1 egg, beaten
1 cup chicken broth
1 1/2 cups milk

If mixture seems a little dry, add more milk or chicken broth. Bake at 350 degrees in a greased casserole dish or wrapped securely in a greased foil packet placed inside the turkey's roasting pan. Time varies depending on the baking method and how many other dishes are stuffed in the oven. If you bake it separately, start checking it after 30 minutes or so.

* * *

**Sour Cream Sugar Cookies**
My paternal great-grandmother always made these at Christmas. We're not sure where she got the recipe, or how far back it goes in the family. The special ingredient is sour cream, which would have been made fresh at the farm back in the day.

While these make tasty cutout cookies, you can also roll the dough in balls and flatten them for no-fuss baking. Frost them with your favorite icing. When January rolls around, I like to make "blizzard cookies" with this recipe. Start with flattened dough balls, bake, then top with cream cheese frosting and flaked coconut!

5 1/2 cups flour (divided)
1/2 teaspoon salt
1 teaspoon baking soda
1 1/2 cups sugar
Sift 4 cups flour and the rest of the dry ingredients in a large bowl.

Cut 1 1/2 cups shortening (3 sticks of margarine) into small cubes and blend into the flour mixture until the crumbs are smaller than the size of a pea. A pastry cutter works well for this.

In a smaller bowl, mix:
½ cup plain sour cream (can use plain or vanilla yogurt in a pinch)
2 eggs
1 teaspoon vanilla

Add the wet ingredients to the dry, blend. Then mix in the last 1 1/2 cups of flour. Don't over mix, or the dough may get tough. Once all the flour is worked in, this is a stiff dough and you might need to use your hands! Chill the dough, then roll out to about 1/4-inch thickness using flour on the work surface and the rolling pin. Bake at 350 degrees, 8 to 10 minutes. Pull them out of the oven when they are dry on top but not yet brown. Cool on wire racks, then frost and/or decorate.

# ABOUT THE NOVELS

*Don't miss any of the titles in the "Growing Season" rural fiction series! All are available in Kindle, paperback, hardcover and large-print paperback formats.*

Melinda is at a crossroads when the "for rent" sign beckons her down a dusty gravel lane. Facing forty, single and downsized from her career at a big-city ad agency, she's struggling to start over when a phone call brings her home to rural Iowa.

She moves to the country, takes on a rundown farm and its headstrong animals, and lands behind the counter of her family's hardware store in the community of Prosper, whose motto is "The Great Little Town That Didn't." And just like the garden she tends under the summer sun, Melinda begins to thrive.

*please turn the page ...*

FIFTH
IN A SERIES

Songbird
Season
❦ a novel ❦

BY MELANIE LAGESCHULTE

SIXTH
IN A
SERIES

The Bright
Season
❦ a novel ❦

BY MELANIE LAGESCHULTE

SEVENTH
IN A SERIES

Turning
Season
❦ a novel ❦

BY MELANIE LAGESCHULTE

EIGHTH
IN A SERIES

The
Blessed
Season
❦ a novel ❦

BY MELANIE LAGESCHULTE

NINTH
IN A
SERIES

Daffodil
Season
❦ a novel ❦

BY MELANIE LAGESCHULTE

TENTH IN A SERIES

Firefly
Season
❦ a novel ❦

BY MELANIE LAGESCHULTE

But when storm clouds arrive on her horizon, can she hold on to the new life she's worked so hard to create? Filled with memorable characters, from a big-hearted farm dog to the weather-obsessed owner of the local co-op, "Growing Season" celebrates the twists and turns of small-town life.

Discover the heartwarming series that's filled with new friends, fresh starts and second chances.

**FOR DETAILS ON THE BOOKS,
VISIT FREMONTCREEKPRESS.COM**

# A SNEAK PEEK
## AT 'GROWING SEASON'

*Here's an exclusive excerpt from the first novel in the series! As we pick up the story, Melinda is discouraged after her job search hasn't turned up anything in Minneapolis. Uncle Frank's heart attack has brought her home to Iowa, and she and Aunt Miriam are waiting at the hospital for word on his condition. Melinda doesn't know it yet, but Miriam has a plan ...*

"Do you know what you are going to do, Melinda?"

Melinda glanced up from the foam cup of coffee she was absentmindedly stirring with one of those tiny plastic straws. It was hospital brew, cheap and hot and bitter, even with two packets of sugar from the cafeteria.

Aunt Miriam plopped down in the beige plastic chair next to Melinda, a wad of tissues in her hand, her brown eyes tired. "It's been, what, a month? Any prospects?"

Melinda had been camped out on her couch, surfing talk shows and house-flipping programs, when her mom had called to tell her about Uncle Frank's heart attack and to ask if she would come home. That was yesterday.

Today they were at the hospital in Mason City, waiting for Frank to come out of surgery. He was going to survive, but needed a triple bypass and lots of rest.

"Well, I'm looking around," Melinda began her standard answer to the question that had been asked more times than she could count in the past month. That included challenging herself with it at least once a day.

"The market's not good. Most of the larger advertising firms in the city aren't hiring. I might get lucky at a smaller company, but most of them have been snapped up by the larger ones. I've got a few more severance checks coming, and then I can apply for unemployment, I guess."

Melinda knew she sounded defeated, bitter, and she hated herself for it. She was healthy, she wasn't starving, the rent was paid.

But some days it had been hard to get up in the morning. Where had the time gone? She wasn't sure, but knew she'd passed too much of it sprawled on her couch, remote in hand.

There were more important things to talk about now. "How is Uncle Frank, what have you heard?"

"The physician's assistant came out about an hour ago to say the bypass is going well." Aunt Miriam folded her hands in a quick praying motion and glanced up at the cream tiles on the waiting-room ceiling. "I'm thankful for that. He'll pull through, thank God. But I don't think he'll be back at the store anytime soon."

Frank and Miriam, who was Melinda's mom's sister,

had owned the hardware store in Prosper, a little community northeast of Swanton, since just after they married. The store had been in Melinda's family ever since her Shrader great-grandparents opened it in 1894. The small town had less than two hundred residents, but Prosper Hardware was its heart. The community's lone gas station had closed more than twenty years ago, and it had been decades since a grocery store operated in the little town.

Prosper Hardware remained the only retail business for ten to fifteen miles, depending on which direction you traveled.

"I know you love the city," Miriam said now, leaning in as if she was sharing a secret, "and you probably can't imagine living out here again. But if you wanted to help me out for awhile, I would really appreciate it."

Melinda took a gulp of her now-lukewarm coffee to buy some time. As much as she loved her parents, she couldn't imagine living with them again. How would she live out of a suitcase, even for a few weeks, when she'd been living on her own for so many years? And what about her life in Minneapolis? But then …

She didn't want to admit it to her aunt, but the last month had been filled with empty days, tears and frustration. Helping out at the store was a chance to drop out of her regular life, which wasn't so great right now. It was the easy way out, a temporary escape, but maybe she was willing to consider it.

"In the meantime," Miriam continued, "can you run

by Prosper Hardware on the way to your parents' house? I need to get an extra set of keys to the staff."

Melinda threaded her way through the antiseptic corridors of the hospital and stepped out into the blindingly bright afternoon sunshine. The bubble of silence inside her car was comforting after the sudden stress of the past two days. She cranked on the air conditioning, leaned back and closed her eyes. It had been weeks since she'd been in the middle of this much activity, and Melinda was surprised by how strange it felt. The woman who had been so busy, who had so much work to do and so many commitments to fill her days and nights, where had she gone?

The chaos of the last twenty-four hours had shown her just how lonely she was, how much she missed the hustle of her former life. She was bored, she could admit to herself now. Bored, and lonely. The longer she was out of a job, the less connected she felt to her old life, her old self. With nothing new on the horizon to replace them, she drifted through the days and weeks, waiting for something to happen.

And now, it had. Melinda opened her eyes and realized she was still clutching the keys to Prosper Hardware in her hand. Then she realized that, for the first time in a long time, she was free to do whatever she wanted. Wherever she wanted.

She made her way out of Mason City, heading east and then south for the forty-five minute drive to Prosper. Platted in the 1890s along a railroad line, the community's founders had big dreams that didn't quite pan out. The irony of the town's name wasn't lost on any of its residents, however. The wooden welcome sign on the edge of the community offered a quaint, colorful painting of Main Street and the town's motto: "Welcome to Prosper, the Great Little Town That Didn't."

There was the inevitable bump-thump as the county highway passed over the railroad tracks just before the local co-op. The blacktop next crossed First Street, made a little diagonal jag to the southeast, and began its three-block run as Prosper's Main Street.

"This is where all the action is," Melinda grinned and shook her head as she rolled into the second block of Main. Prosper Hardware crowned the middle of the block on her right, a two-story, red brick building with limestone-block details above its windows and on its corners. Display windows flanked both sides of its dark-green front door. A matching green awning sheltered the first floor from the ever-changing Iowa weather.

This block was dotted with benches made of black iron scrollwork and warm wood slats, encouraging visitors and residents to stop for a chat and soak up the little town's welcoming atmosphere. Hanging baskets of purple and white impatiens danced in the early-summer breeze on decorative iron hooks installed on the light poles. Miriam had rallied the business community a few years ago to get both projects completed, and Melinda suspected her aunt had pulled a large chunk of the cost from her own pocket. A squat, gray stone building between Prosper Hardware and Third Street housed the town's post office. Right across from the hardware store stood Prosper City Hall and the next-door library.

As Melinda got out of the car, not bothering to click the door locks, she thought about how urban residents always bragged about city life, that everything was so convenient and all the neighborhoods had their own shops within walking distance of most people's homes.

"It's no different here," she said, feeling the blast of summer heat radiating off the asphalt-coated street. "Get your mail, pick up some nails and grab a free book, all within about a hundred feet."

She craned her neck to see to the end of Main, down past the Catholic church. The dark-green building with the gleaming white trim was still the home of Prosper Veterinary Services. There was an adorable black-and-white calf, its red halter tied to a yard stake, munching the emerald-green grass under the front lawn's oak tree.

The shade cast by Prosper Hardware's awning was inviting. Melinda was tempted to flop down on one of the benches out front, close her eyes for a minute or two. But it had been three years since she had last been inside the store. She was curious to see if anything had changed at Prosper Hardware, and secretly hoped it hadn't.

*Find "Growing Season" and its sequels at Amazon.com, or order them through your favorite bookstore. All the novels are available in Kindle, paperback, hardcover and large-print paperback formats.*

CPSIA information can be obtained
at www.ICGtesting.com
Printed in the USA
LVHW110319021122
732180LV00013B/107

9 780998 863856